Other Collins Red Storybooks to enjoy

The Dream Snatcher

Kara May

Illustrated by Amanda Harvey

CollinsChildren'sBooks

An imprint of HarperCollinsPublishers

First published in Great Britain by Collins in 1997
First published in paperback by Collins in 1998
Collins is an imprint of HarperCollins *Publishers* Ltd
77-85 Fulham Palace Road, Hammersmith, London, W6 8JB

1 3 5 7 9 8 6 4 2

Text copyright © Kara May 1997
Illustrations copyright © Amanda Harvey 1997

ISBN 0 00 675253 5

The author and illustrator assert the moral right to be identified as
the author and illustrator of the work.

Printed and bound in Great Britain by Caledonian International Book
Manufacturing Ltd, Glasgow G64

CHAPTER ONE

The Stranger's Offer

The Stranger came striding into the town. Jodie saw the mud on his boots and knew he must have come over the fields. She jumped aside to let him pass.

"Who is he?" she wondered. He had a large bag with metal studs that sent off fiery sparks as they caught the sun. And his clothes! He was wearing: a long cloak wrapped tightly around him

a wide brimmed hat that hid his face in shadow

and red hobnail boots!

She'd lived in the small town all her life and she'd never seen anyone like him. She was surprised others hadn't noticed him too. Not that he noticed her! He swished his cloak more tightly

around him and headed into the shopping centre.

"I haven't any money to buy anything. I won't go in," decided Jodie. She hovered outside, curiously puzzling about the Stranger.

The shopping centre was new, only just finished, and it towered tall, all concrete and glass. Four steps led to the huge square doorway and people were streaming in from all over town. On the top floor was a car park that made Jodie think of a concrete wart! Just the look of it made her shudder. But now, someone was up there, leaning over the ledge between the low car park wall and the roof. She knew by the hat it was the Stranger. He must have gone to look at the view from up there. She'd heard you could see all the town.

"Oh no! What's he doing!" gasped Jodie.

The Stranger was climbing out onto the ledge. Lots of others noticed him now! They emptied out of the shopping centre and came from all round to see what was up. Iodie saw her family there with the rest, pointing up at the Stranger as he stood on the ledge, stone-still.

"He's showing off!" people were saying.

"Or maybe he's going to jump!"

"Oi you!" shouted Alf the Butcher.

The Stranger raised a clenched fist.

"I'm living here now!" he bellowed.

"You can't live in our car park," bellowed back the people.

The Stranger went to say something further but they cut him short with a shout. "Come down at once! That car park's our property!"

"Let's go get him!" urged Alf the Butcher.

Before Alf and the others could take a step, the Stranger leapt back into the car park. Then he was back! He held a metallic red car over his head. He gave a wild roar and hurled it over the ledge.

"Here comes the next! I said I'd live here and I mean what I say!"

Jodie watched, wide-eyed, as one after another cars plummeted down like metal birds that had lost their wings. It was such an extraordinary sight she was more intrigued than afraid, but the others were terrified.

What would the Stranger do next? they trembled.

He could have a gun...

Or a bomb!

"Mark my words, he'll be threatening and wanting something! Our money like as not!" said Alf the Butcher.

"I've more money than you all put together!" boomed out the Stranger. "What I want— But I'll come down! Wait!" he commanded.

Jodie noticed that no one moved, not even Alf. It was as if the Stranger's words weighted them down to the spot. His hobnail boots thudded through the deserted shopping centre. He was getting closer. Then, there he was! The pulse in her throat beat fast. He looked as if he had thunder inside him and it might burst out any minute. She wasn't curious now, but afraid. She turned to run and saw with dismay all the people of the town seemed to have gathered, packed in a crowd tightly around her. There was no way she could make her way through them but she determined she'd go the first chance she got.

The Stranger stood on the top step. His fierce presence seemed to fill the doorway. He lifted the bag down from his shoulder. Fearing what might be in it, the crowd drew back like a wave from a rock.

"It's not a bomb," he sneered. "But if I wanted—" He snapped his fingers. "I could blow up your town like that! No, what I want..."

His words hung in the air.

They held their breaths.

"What I want are your dreams," said the Stranger.

"Our dreams!" echoed Jodie.

"Dreams aren't like lamb chops. You can't wrap 'em in newspaper and hand 'em over!" said Alf the Butcher.

The people started to laugh. "He's a nutter! All boots and cloak and hat! And now he's wanting our dreams!"

Jodie caught sight of the stranger's face under the brim of his hat. His mouth was tightened in an angry line. His forehead was furrowed in frowns. She went to warn them not to make fun of him. Before she could speak, he stamped his foot.

"I mean what I say! Look!" he snarled out.

They turned towards him as if pulled by an invisible string. All eyes were fixed upon him as the Stranger reached into his cloak. He took out a round box-like gadget about sixteen centimetres across. At first sight it seemed to be made of silver but then it was suddenly red, then orange, yellow, then blues and violet, then all colours together.

"It picks up dreams out of the air," he said. "It can pick up your dreams like a

television picks up real-life things so you can see and hear them."

"A Dream Box!" breathed Jodie. "How brilliant!"

"I invented it," the Stranger went on with a shrug, as if that was of no importance. "I'll pay a good price for your dreams," he added.

Excited now, the people whispered:

"He's bananas, of course..."

"Dreams are good for nothing..."

"You can't wear them!"

"You can't live in them either!"

"If you tried wearing them, you'd have nothing on!"

"But he said he'd pay..."

"How much will you pay?" they demanded.

The Stranger smiled but so coldly that Jodie shivered. Again she turned to go but she was still trapped by the crowd and she watched as he reached down into the bag beside him. He pulled out a small plastic cup. He raised his other hand over it and gold coins flowed from his long fingers and filled it to the brim.

"I'll pay a cup of gold coins to anyone who'll sell me their dreams. I must have one dream at least, every night for a year. That's the deal. What do you say? Yes or no?"

"A cup of gold coins!" ooh-aahed the people.

"They'll be worth a small fortune!"

"Not only that, they'll keep their value!"

"If they're the real thing," said Alf.

The Stranger turned sharply towards him. "I don't deal in cheap metal trash! But see for yourself." He tossed a coin to Alf who bit it hard to test it. The people saw from his face it was the real thing.

"As I told you before, I mean what I say!" said the Stranger. He held up his hand to show a square of red plastic that fitted into his palm. "Touch it just once and the deal between us is sealed. I get your dreams and you get your gold!

Who'll sell me their dreams?" he roared out.

He didn't have to ask again! The crowd surged forward with hands outstretched.

"I'll sell! I'll sell! I'll sell!"

Their frenzied shouts filled the air.

Even the children pushed and shoved, eager to get their cups of gold.

All except Jodie.

Never sell your dreams, Jodie's gran had told her. She could hear her voice as if she were speaking now.

The crowd elbowed Jodie this way and that but she didn't notice, she was thinking of her gran. She'd lived with her gran since her parents had died when she was too young to remember them. Then not long ago, her gran had died too.

"I wish you were here, Gran," she whispered.

Her gran had made their little tumbledown house so cosy and she always knew exactly the thing to brighten Jodie up when she felt upset about something. Her gran might dance about, even on the bed. That soon had her laughing! Or often her gran would sing so she'd feel calm inside like the calmest sea. And sometimes her gran—

"But Gran is dead. There's no point in thinking back," thought Jodie.

Now she lived at her uncle's. She worked about the house but if there was money to spare for a treat, her cousins, being older, always came first; when her turn came, the money had somehow run out. She had to wear her cousins' hand-me-downs which never quite fitted and other children made fun of her.

"But if I sell my dreams...! A cup of gold," glowed Jodie. "Just think what I could do with that! I'd have the smartest and lots of everything. No one'd make fun of me then! Never, ever again!"

Her gran wouldn't want her to miss

out on a chance like this! More than anyone, Gran had wanted her to be happy.

She began to make her way forward with the others. Already her cousins were shoving their way through the crowd that jostled around the Stranger.

"One at a time!" he growled. "There's gold enough for you all."

She noticed he had that sneering look on his face as he handed the cup of gold to Alf, who was now at the top of the queue. The Stranger still looked angry and fierce although he was getting the promise of dreams that he wanted.

"My dreams make me laugh like Gran could do," thought Jodie. Not that her *nightmares* were funny, she shivered, with monsters that chased and threatened to eat her! But then there were dreams so extraordinary they filled her with wonder. She'd miss them. They were something truly her own.

She glanced towards the Stranger. He was scowling and stamping about.

"I can't let him have my dreams. I can't and that's that."

Her decision was suddenly clear in her mind. She longed for the cup of gold but she'd just have to do without.

Quickly, Jodie turned to go.

The Stranger saw her. "Wait, girl!"

His voice was so heavy his words struck like a blow. Jodie wanted to run. But she was too afraid not to obey him.

CHAPTER TWO

Jodie Nobody

Jodie stood with her fists gripped by her sides and she lowered her eyes as the Stranger came towards her.

"What's your name, girl?" he rasped.

"My name is Jodie," she whispered.

She was aware that everyone was staring at her. Not just the Stranger but the people too. A sudden hush fell. She was desperate for something to fill it.

"Please, what's *your* name?" she blurted.

The Stranger started. "My name!" he growled. "You ask my name, girl!"

"She'll be in for it now! She's made him angry," muttered the people.

Jodie gripped her fists more tightly and waited for the blasting to come. But when at last the Stranger spoke, his voice wasn't angry. It sounded flat and dull as if the feeling were all drained out.

"You can call me the Dream Snatcher," he said with a shrug. "Why not? It's what I do. But enough of all this! To business, girl," the Dream Snatcher rapped out abruptly. "A cup of gold for your dreams. Is it a deal? Yes or no?"

He took it she'd answer "yes" and he

held out the cup of gold. Jodie didn't dare refuse and she reached out her hand to take it. Like a flame of fire, her gran's warning burst into her mind:

Never sell your dreams.

She'd always meant to ask her gran, why not? It was too late for that now. But one thing was certain, thought Jodie. Her gran had never let her down or harmed her, not once, not ever.

She took a deep breath.

"My dreams are not for sale," she said.

The people gasped.

"Hmph! Please yourself, girl," said the Dream Snatcher.

That was it!

He waved her off.

Jodie couldn't believe it. She took her chance and fled.

She ran home and went to her room till

she saw her family come down the street. They were all clutching their cups of gold. She'd never seen her uncle look so happy but when he saw her, he greeted her with a stony stare.

"So, here's the little miss who had her chance to be rich and turned up her nose at it."

"But," began Jodie. She wanted to tell him what her gran had told her. Her uncle cut her short.

"Don't ask me for a hand-out. You won't get it, Miss!"

"Don't go asking us either!" chimed in her cousins. "You're not getting your mitts on our money."

"I wasn't going to ask," answered Jodie, and went back to her room.

That night when the moon was up, Jodie

stirred in her sleep and suddenly woke. She got up and went to the window.

"The Dream Snatcher! Here he comes!"

She watched as he came down the street. He held the Dream Box over his head, turning it this way and that. She saw it flash with colours as it snatched up the dreams from the people as they slept.

"What will he do with them?" she wondered. She was still wondering as she went back to bed.

In a dream of her own, she saw the Dream Snatcher make his way through the shopping centre up to the car park. A screen ran the full length of one wall. There was an assortment of gadgets underneath it. He slotted the Dream Box into one of them. At once a red rabbit appeared on the screen. It was standing on its head, eating a banana and wearing a skirt made of cabbage leaves! Whose dream was it? Jodie smiled in her sleep. Alf the Butcher's perhaps!

She saw one dream after another flash onto the screen. Sad dreams, weird dreams, funny dreams, cruel dreams. The Dream Snatcher watched them all, stretched out on the cold concrete floor.

At last the screen went blank. He hauled himself to his feet and began to stamp about.

That was the last thing Jodie remembered when she woke next morning. She was sure what she'd seen had truly happened. But she had a question that she put to her uncle.

"Why does the Dream Snatcher buy other people's dreams?" she asked. "Why doesn't he dream his own?"

"Who cares!" snorted her uncle. "What he does is up to him. We've got our money and we're going to spend it."

"Spend! Spend! Spend!" shrieked her cousins.

Her uncle clapped his hands. "To the shopping centre! Let's go!"

Jodie watched as they went running gleefully down the street. All over the town it was the same. People went on a spend! spend! spend! bonanza. They installed the newest appliances into their homes, bought flashy cars, designer clothes, clever gadgets, whatever they fancied. The children filled their cupboards with toys and splashed out on computers and mountain bikes and paraded around in the latest gear.

All except Jodie.

She was still wearing her cousins' hand-me downs.

The other children had often picked on her, even when her gran was alive. There was no stopping them now.

"A scarecrow looks smarter than you!" they jeered. "You haven't even got your own TV or computer. You're a nobody, Jodie!"

"Jodie Nobody! Jodie Nobody!"

They danced around her and chanted it, over and over. Her cousins joined in.

"You've no one to blame but yourself," said her uncle. "You could have been as rich as the rest of us. But no, you'd sooner have your dreams which are no use to man or beast!"

Jodie went again to explain about her gran's warning but no one was listening.

Her cousins sniggered, "Jodie Nobody."

It became a nickname that everyone called her.

Her uncle treated her as if he still hadn't a penny. She had mostly bread and butter to eat with not even jam for a treat. He did up the house and even built a patio and extension but he left her room as it was, with a bare wooden floor and a crack in the window where the wind howled in.

"You can dream yourself warm, Jodie Nobody," smirked her cousins. "We're going shopping."

The shopping centre began to open all night, and also the pubs and restaurants. People went from one to the other. There was no point in going to bed, they never

really slept. Since they'd sold their dreams it was as if a part of them was missing and they tossed and turned all night, trying to find it. But they weren't too bothered.

"If we can't sleep, we'll shop and have fun instead. After all, we can afford it."

Her cousins told Jodie they were having a party.

"We've got a new sound system," they crowed. "It'll be the best party ever!"

"I'll help you get things ready. Please may I come?" she asked.

They looked at her as if she were something yucky that had crawled out from under a stone.

"You've got to be joking! We don't want you at our party, Jodie Nobody. Keep out or else!"

They locked her in her room when the party started. Jodie sat on her bed, too miserable even to put on the light. To cheer herself up she went over last night's funny dream where she wasn't herself, but an ostrich! She'd buried her head not in the sand, but in a freezer. Then the ice melted and—

Suddenly she heard footsteps out in the street.

"The Dream Snatcher! I knew he'd come! He hasn't missed a night yet."

Jodie ran to the window. The Dream Snatcher was shaking the Dream Box as if it were a clock he was trying to make tick. It flashed slowly once or twice. Jodie wasn't surprised! With the music from the party throbbing over the roof tops, it'd be hard for people to sleep, never mind dream.

The Dream Snatcher thrust the Dream Box into his pocket.

And looked up.

And saw her.

She was always careful to hide behind the curtain when she watched him go by. But with the party going on, she'd forgotten.

What should she do?

Was it up to her so say "hullo!" or something?

The words froze in her throat.

She just stared.

The Dream Snatcher stared back.

At last he strode off.

"Whew!" breathed Jodie.

She went back and sat on her bed and listened to the shouts and whoops of laughter. It seemed all the town was at the party except for her... and the Dream Snatcher.

CHAPTER THREE

The Dream Snatcher's Threat

The all-night parties went on and so did the spend! spend! spend! bonanza. But the lack of sleep began to take its toll. People grew pale-faced and weary. All over the town it was yawn! yawn! yawn! After a while no one had the strength to take pleasure in anything, not even spending money – if they had any left.

But that wasn't the worst of it.

Now they couldn't sleep, they couldn't dream either, and they'd promised the Dream Snatcher at least one dream a night. They tried to make up day-dreams in the hope he'd accept them instead. But their minds stayed stubbornly blank. They couldn't understand it. Since they'd made the deal to sell their dreams, sleep took itself off and no dreams would come either.

"It's a mystery," they yawned, but they were much too tired to puzzle it out.

To cheer themselves up, they told each other it was just a passing phase.

"Our dreams will come back when they're good and ready. The Dream Snatcher will have to wait till then."

Even so, they stayed shut in their houses, not just because they were too tired to go out, but to avoid the Dream Snatcher.

Again and again, Jodie thought of her gran. If it hadn't been for Gran's warning, she'd be a sleepless zombie like the others. But she felt uneasy about what the Dream Snatcher might do and miserable, too. No one in the town would talk to her, especially not her family who disliked her even more now she woke fresh from a night's sleep and *they* couldn't sleep a wink.

"Oh well, at least I've got my dreams," sighed Jodie.

The previous night she'd dreamt a whale took her to the bottom of the ocean. What a dream that was! A circus of clowns jumped out of a shell and put on the craziest show. She and the whale were rolling around with laughter. Then a spaceman arrived. How he got there she couldn't remember. She'd try to think later. It was so hot in the house, she had to get outdoors.

Her family were slumped in front of the television, not exactly asleep or awake. She was sad to see them in such

a state but it did no good to say anything. Their tempers were frayed by tiredness. They were always shouting and arguing and needed no excuse to turn their bad tempers on her. The weather made things worse. It had turned into a blazing summer. The heat burned through the house like an unseen fire.

Jodie slipped out through the front door. She'd taught herself to open it noiselessly so as not to attract her family's attention. They didn't want her around but they didn't want her to leave the house either.

She ran on down the path. It was barely cooler outside. Sometimes she walked in the fields but the sun had withered the grass; they were scorched and barren. Mostly she walked in the centre of town. The streets were usually deserted and she enjoyed wandering among the tall buildings. They were calming, somehow, so solid and still, and she could always shelter in the shade of their doorways.

She was careful, as always, not to venture near the shopping centre but she was aware of the Dream Snatcher's presence. She wondered why he chose to live in the car park. He had loads of money, it couldn't be that he was hard up.

"Maybe he's not bothered where he lives," she thought. "A car park's the same to him as anywhere, and of course from up there he can see all the town."

Jodie strolled on through the empty streets. Dusk was falling. But the Dream Snatcher was out early this evening. She caught the sound of hobnail boots. They struck the pavement so hard they set up an echo between the buildings. She

couldn't tell which way he was coming. If she ran the wrong way, she panicked, she could find herself meeting him face to face.

She made a dash for the nearest doorway and she crouched down in its darkest corner.

"He's coming!"

The Dream Snatcher was muttering savagely under his breath. He thrashed at the air with the Dream Box. But no, he hadn't seen her.

She waited till he was out of earshot. Now she had to get home as fast as she could and warn her uncle that the Dream Snatcher was angry.

"It's not your fault your dreams have stopped," she said. "If you went to him and explained—"

Her uncle interrupted her with a shake

of his fist. "When I want your advice, Miss, I'll ask for it."

"M.Y.O.B. Mind your own business, Nosey Jodie Nobody." Her cousins flexed their fingers, ready to pinch. Jodie dodged past just in time. She ran up to her room and locked the door behind her.

A few days later, Jodie was woken by a fearsome roar.

"The Dream Snatcher!" she whispered.

He roared out again through a loudspeaker and summoned the people to the shopping centre.

"We don't have to do as he says," said her uncle.

All through the town, people were saying the same and remained in their houses and shut the windows and closed the curtains.

The third time, the Dream Snatcher's

voice burst through the town like a dynamite blast. They remembered what he'd done to the cars on the first day he'd arrived in town.

"May as well see what he wants," they said.

Jodie watched as her uncle led the rest of the family down the street. Her cousins followed him, slow as reluctant snails.

"What should I do?" she wondered. She decided she'd better go too and followed along behind them.

The Dream Snatcher was pacing the top step to the shopping centre. He shook the Dream Box at the people gathered below.

"Night after night I return without a single dream! I kept my side of the deal," he roared. "I expect you to keep yours!"

They rushed to explain that they'd meant, truly meant, to keep their side of the deal.

"Dream Snatcher, honestly, we never expected our dreams to run out!"

"That is your problem not mine," he spat back at them. "If you can't keep your side of the deal, give back the money I paid you."

But the money was gone. In fact, *all* their money was gone.

"We've been too tired to work. We've had to spend our savings," they said.

"You can see, we're half dead on our feet."

"We're sure to fall asleep soon. Then we can dream the dreams we owe you. Please, give us more time!"

The Dream Snatcher shook his fists and gnashed his teeth. He looked as if there was a volcano inside him and it was about to erupt on them.

"Very well," he said at last. His voice was calm and steady but with a sharp edge that cut into the air. It made them tremble even more than his ranting and roaring.

"You've got three more days and nights," he went on. "If by then there are no dreams in the Dream Box, I will blast your town to dust and blow that dust to the corners of the earth so no trace of the town remains."

Jodie knew he meant what he said and saw everyone was wild-eyed with fear. They drew together for comfort. She was as scared as they but there was no point in her saying so. She ran home and she lay on her bed and wept.

That night as darkness fell, the people tried every sleep-making device they knew so they could dream some dreams and save their town.

They drank milky drinks.

They ate cheese and pickle.

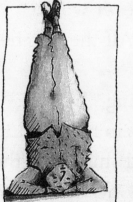

They stood on their heads.

They counted sheep. All they got were headaches and tummy aches.

The next night it was the same.

As the third night fell, they met together in the school hall at the end of Jodie's street. They were in a terrible panic.

"We've not got a dream between us!"

"He'll blow up the town, there's no stopping him!"

"He'll find a way, whatever we do."

Then someone, it was Alf the Butcher in fact, remembered Jodie.

"This is what I'm thinking," he said.

He told them what was in his mind.

Jodie's uncle clapped him on the shoulder. "Well done," he said. "I'd forgotten about that little miss. There's no time to be lost. Let's go!"

He led the way towards the house and the people followed behind him.

CHAPTER FOUR

Jodie's Answer

Jodie stirred in her sleep. She suddenly sat up with a gasp of panic and looked wildly round her.

"Who... what is it...!"

She blinked as the light went on to see her uncle glowering down at her.

"Our town faces ruin! But you're

sleeping and dreaming! Get up at once, Miss! The people are waiting."

Jodie grabbed a dressing gown and followed her uncle into the street.

"Please, what is it? What can I do?"

"Shut your mouth and listen. What you will do is this," said her uncle. "You'll go to the Dream Snatcher, now, at once, and say you'll give him your dreams, free and for nothing. It's the one hope we have to spare our town!"

The people closed in around her.

"You heard what your uncle said, Miss."

Her uncle raised his fist. "You'll do as I say, or—"

Before he could say what he would do, the Dream Snatcher appeared from behind the crowd.

"I heard all that. Come here, girl."

Eager to smarm up to the Dream

Snatcher, the people made a path for her.

"Do as he says, Miss."

Jodie just stood, too frightened to move. She kept her eyes down. All the same she saw the Dream Snatcher, a dark shadow outlined in lamplight, painted onto the pavement.

To her relief he didn't come any closer and left several metres between them.

"I want nothing for nothing," he said. "Sell me your dreams, girl, and I'll pay not one but two cups of gold *and* I'll spare the town."

"Two cups of gold!" the people cried. "We only got one."

But this wasn't the time to fret about that.

They moved towards Jodie.

"Sell your dreams! Save our town!"

Jodie opened her mouth to say "yes" but

her gran's warning came back with such force that the word froze in her throat.

The people started to stamp their feet. "Sell! Sell! Sell!"

"Say you agree," her uncle hissed and gave her arm a squeeze.

"Let her be!" whipped out the Dream Snatcher. He turned towards Jodie. "You've got till first light tomorrow to give me your answer, yes or no. As for the rest of you, harm one hair of her head in the meantime, and you will perish along with your town."

He headed off down the street, leaving Jodie staring after him.

The people whispered, "For all she seems meek as a dove, that little miss has a will of her own." They remembered the Dream Snatcher's threat. "We daren't force her to do as we say. Let's try tears instead!"

Some had to pinch themselves to make the tears come as weeping and wailing, they flocked around Jodie.

"Please, Jodie, dear Jodie, *please!* (sob! sob!) Sell your dreams and save our town."

Jodie longed to agree. The longing was like an ache in her heart. But she couldn't forget her gran's warning or what had happened to everyone else when they'd sold their dreams.

"But if I don't," she thought, "the town will be destroyed. What shall I do?" she silently asked, over and over. "I'll sleep on it," she decided at last. "The Dream Snatcher gave me till morning to give him my answer."

The people couldn't wait. "We want this settled at once, Miss. We're taking you to him right now. You can make up your mind on the way."

Jodie felt fingers grip her arms and prod her back. They gripped and prodded till they reached the shopping centre.

"A word before you go," the people breathed in her ear. "If you let us down and refuse his offer, you'll regret it, Miss."

They gave her a push.

The huge door shut SLAM! behind her.

Jodie just stood, very still.

The shopping centre was quiet, so quiet she could hear the pulse in her head. It was dark, too, except for the light of the moon that cast shifting shadows around her. She watched them for a while. Not knowing what else to do, she began to make her way up to the car park. She walked quietly, pausing on every step, to get there as slowly as possible.

She expected the Dream Snatcher to

come striding towards her. But where was he? She looked around and shivered. The car park was just as she'd seen it that first night in her dream, a cold, bleak place and damp, too, even on the hot summer night.

Jodie saw the Dream Snatcher now. He was lying scrunched up on the concrete floor in front of the blank screen. The Dream Box was tossed on the floor beside him. He realised Jodie was looking at him.

"I didn't hear you come, girl. I wasn't expecting you so soon."

He looked embarrassed at being caught unawares and to her astonishment he blushed! It was only for half a moment but even so, when he came towards her with his usual sneering scowl, she didn't feel quite so scared of him.

"Please," she burst out, "may I ask you a question?"

"First you want to know my name. Now another question," he growled. "Get on with it then. What is it?"

"Why do you want to buy my dreams? Why not save your money and dream your own?" There! She'd asked him, the question that had puzzled her from the start.

The Dream Snatcher swept his cloak around him and gave a low, moaning howl. From the look on his face Jodie was afraid he was going to strike her but he struck the side of his head.

"I don't know how to dream!" he roared out. "What do you say to that?"

Jodie was too startled to say anything!

To her relief, when he spoke again, he was calmer.

"For as long as I can remember," he said, "I've wanted to know what it's like to go to sleep at night and dream. It's like having a thirst nothing else can quench. Other people's dreams are better than none. But you'd know nothing of that!" he broke off. His eyes burned at Jodie.

"Will you sell me your dreams, girl, yes or no?"

She tried to think. If only her thoughts would stay still a moment! If only she could tell one thought from the other!

"My mind's all of a muddle," she trembled. "It might help me decide what to do if you sing to me. That's what my gran would do."

"Your gran!"

"Yes, my gran," quivered Jodie.

The Dream Snatcher gave that laugh with a sneer. "I dare say your gran sang like a bird. But me? You'd do better to ask a dog to sprout himself wings and fly!"

Jodie looked at him in surprise. "But it's easy to sing. I'll show you." Talking about her gran had somehow made her feel less afraid.

She told him to open his mouth very wide. "Now make the *highest* note that you can."

The Dream Snatcher glared at her savagely.

"Very well then, if I must," he muttered. "If it'll help you to give me your answer."

He opened his mouth wide, as Jodie had told him.

"LAAAAA!" he went, very high.

"Now make the *lowest* note that you can."

He made a low rumbling "laaaaah."

"Now make a note in between," urged Jodie.

He took a big breath.

"Laaaaa."

She gave him just enough time to catch his breath. "Now sing the notes one after the other, the high and the low and the one in between."

"Like this?" asked the Dream Snatcher.

"Laaaaa! Laaaaa! Laaaaah!"

"Again!" said Jodie. "But faster."

He did as she said.

"Don't stop," put in Jodie. "Keep going."

He made the three notes come faster and faster till they tripped off his tongue, and soon other notes slipped in as well. He sang on, a bewildered look on his face, as if each note was unexpected. Jodie listened and felt somewhat soothed. She wondered what he'd do with her dreams if she sold them? And what would happen to her if she did!

But now the Dream Snatcher had stopped singing. What should she tell him? To her dismay, the muddle in her mind had turned into a fog.

"My answer must be there some-where," she quaked. "It might help me to find it if you dance for me. That's what my gran would do."

"You're making fun of me, girl!"

The Dream Snatcher stamped so hard with his hobnail boots a crack ran over the concrete floor.

"Your gran no doubt had dainty feet!

My feet are clodhoppers! They can stride and stamp! But dance?" he bellowed. "You'd do better to ask a brute of a bear to leap into the air and fly."

Jodie saw the flush of anger rush over his face. She wanted to run. But she thought of the people waiting outside. She made herself take a long slow breath.

"It's easy to dance," she said at last. "I'll try to show you how."

Using all her strength, she lifted his hefty right foot and lowered it down to the ground so the hobnail boot made a loud TAP!

Next she raised and lowered his left foot so that, too, made a loud TAP.

"Now you do it, by yourself," she said.

The Dream Snatcher turned his back on her, but slowly he raised his right foot.

TAP!

He went on too quickly. As he raised his left foot he lost his balance. Jodie reached out to stop his fall. Too late! He crashed head first to the ground with a cry of such fury she felt the force of it, hot as burning wind. The people heard it below.

"She has said no! We are lost!" they moaned, and huddled closer together.

CHAPTER FIVE

The Dream Snatcher and the Silver Flute

The Dream Snatcher lay on the floor where he'd fallen. Jodie knew he was angry with himself for being clumsy, and might well turn his anger on her. One wrong move or one wrong word and he'd go for her. She mustn't give him the chance but it took all her effort to keep her voice steady.

"Try it again," she said.

The Dream Snatcher snarled. He grumbled and mumbled and his face furrowed in frowns as he hauled himself up. Grunting, he held himself straight, raised his left foot and lowered it.

TAP!

Then he did the same with his right foot.

TAP!

"Now faster!" said Jodie, and she crossed her fingers and held her breath.

He danced up and down and round and round. His feet kept up a rhythm and didn't trip over themselves or falter once.

"But, that's brilliant!" said Jodie.

She watched as he danced on, *tappity, tap*. She felt calmer now and again she asked herself, what shall I do? She went

through the arguments yet again:

"When you think of it, dreams are just unreal things I see in my sleep. Of course, the Dream Snatcher can have them."

But a moment later:

"I don't care what my dreams are or aren't, I know I'd miss them! And besides, Gran told me..." But Gran didn't know about the Dream Snatcher!

"And she didn't know about my uncle and everyone. How they'll hate me more than ever or worse if I don't do as they want. And I should, I must, so the town will be safe."

But if she said "yes" to the Dream Snatcher's offer...

"I'll end up all frazzled, the same as the others!"

Whatever the answer, she or the town would be the worse for it. But for now, she'd rest, just for a second or two.

Jodie didn't know how long she sat there but her mind was no longer muddled or foggy. It was as clear as glass. She saw a word begin to write itself, like on a computer screen. The Dream Snatcher saw the look on her face.

"You've got your answer!" he whooped. "Is it yes or no?"

As soon as he spoke, Jodie's mind seemed to shatter in pieces. If only he'd waited, just half a minute! "My answer was there, I'm sure of it, but you startled it off. I've lost it!"

The Dream Snatcher threw himself in a corner and began to moan.

As if that noise would bring back my answer, thought Jodie. Well, let him get on with it. All her strength was drained out of her. All she wanted to do was sleep.

She turned away and buried her head in her hands.

"Will it help if I sing or dance?" ventured the Dream Snatcher at last.

"My mind's a blank. But maybe if you play some music." She expected another bellowing outburst, but to her surprise he didn't even shout.

"Hmph! I suppose that's what your gran would do! This gran of yours, I dare say, played like an angel!"

"Yes, as a matter of fact, she did," answered Jodie.

"So what did she play, this granny-angel?"

"The recorder. She gave it to me before she died. I've got it at home. If you want, I'll fetch it."

"No need for that! Come with me!"

The Dream Snatcher took her down to

the music shop on the floor below. He stared at the shelf of recorders.

"Which one shall I have?" he asked.

Jodie chose a recorder for him, and they returned to the car park.

"I don't know why I'm bothering. I've no ear for music." To prove his point, the Dream Snatcher pressed his lips to the mouthpiece and what came out was a hideous screech.

Jodie covered her ears.

"There! I told you, girl! I'd go floating about on a cloud before I got a note out of this thing!"

He flung the recorder aside.

Jodie picked it up.

"You don't just blow," she said wearily. "You use your fingers too." She played a few notes, silvery and pure, and gave the recorder back to him. The next note he made wasn't exactly sweet but nor was it a hideous screech.

"I'll try again," he offered.

This time the note was true. He played another and another and another and at last they formed themselves into a simple tune.

"That wasn't too bad," he said with a grin. "I'll see if I can play it again, only better."

Jodie sat back and listened, but she kept an eye on him. He might lose patience and fly into one of his rages. She felt the music sweep over her. She leant back against the concrete wall. She'd give herself just a few minutes, then she'd try again to think of her answer.

The minutes passed and she saw the first light of morning spread a pale gold gleam on the concrete floor.

The Dream Snatcher yawned. "I had something to ask you, girl," he said sleepily. Before he recalled what it was, he yawned again and sank down on the floor beside her. His eyes closed. Jodie saw with relief he'd fallen asleep. But not for long. He sat up with a start.

"I thought I was singing," he said.

"You *did* sing, before," said Jodie.

He nodded, and slept again.

But again, not for long.

"I thought I saw myself dancing, tappity-tap."

"You *did* dance, before."

"So I did!" he grinned to himself, and went back to sleep.

How Jodie longed to sleep too. But she knew that she mustn't. It was morning. Her time was up.

She saw the Dream Snatcher stir.

He leapt to his feet.

He was wide awake now.

Now he'd want her answer!

Jodie drew back against the wall as if she could press herself safely inside. Her heart beat fast as a terrified bird's. But the Dream Snatcher seemed not to see her. He was pacing the car park, round and round, muttering wildly under his breath. Again and again he struck his head with his fists.

He suddenly strode over and stood before Jodie. She saw his eyes were wild with fear.

"Tell me, girl, where am I?" he trembled. "Am I in the car park? Yes or no?"

Jodie nodded. "Yes," she whispered.

"But just now, I thought I was out in the fields."

"In the fields?" she exclaimed.

"What's more," he burst out, "I thought I was playing not the recorder here in my hand, but a silver flute, and the trees rose up by their roots and danced, and the leaves sang!"

He gripped her by the shoulders. His hands were shaking. "Have I lost my mind! I want the truth, girl. Yes or no!"

Before Jodie could answer he turned

away and raged around the car park.

"I always feared I'd go off my head and now I have! I don't need you to tell me that. Dancing trees and singing leaves! What craziness next I wonder. The people are to blame!" he thundered. "They broke their promise, they—"

Jodie put her hand on his arm.

"It was a dream," she said. "You were dreaming."

For a long time they both just stood, too amazed to say anything further.

CHAPTER SIX

The Dream Snatcher's Garden

Sunbeams flitted over the floor of the car park, up the walls and across the ceiling. The Dream Snatcher watched them. Then he turned to Jodie.

"You taught me to dream, girl," he said.

Jodie was as astonished as he. "If I

did, I don't quite know how."

"Never mind how," he laughed. "For what you've done for me, you can have what you want! Name your own price, girl! Whatever you want!"

Jodie didn't pause, not for a second.

"Please," she said, "I'd like you to spare the town."

The laughter left the Dream Snatcher's face. "The people broke their part of the deal. I can't forgive that!"

"You asked what I wanted—"

"But I meant—"

"That's what I want," cut in Jodie. "I want you to spare the town."

"But why? I know how the people have treated you. Why ask a favour for them?"

"This is my town and that is that," replied Jodie.

The Dream Snatcher remembered he'd

said he'd spare the town in return for her dreams, but she'd given him much more than that.

"You shall have what you want," he said. "Though I have to say, I don't understand."

Jodie was so relieved she could only stammer, "Thank you." She didn't know what to do next so she held out her hand and the Dream Snatcher shook it.

"But I must pay you," he said. He began to conjure cups of gold coins out of the air.

"No, please!" said Jodie. His money had done no one else any good and she didn't want it.

The Dream Snatcher put the gold in his pocket and stared at her with a puzzled frown.

"Look," he burst out. "I want to give you something that's just for you. If you won't let me pay you, may I give you a gift? I can't think exactly what," he rushed on, "but as soon as I do you shall have it. There now!"

"That'd be lovely," said Jodie.

"We've agreed on something at last!"

They started to laugh and couldn't stop. It was as if bubbles were fizzing round inside them.

The Dream Snatcher gave an excited whoop. "I want to see how the world looks now I can make music and sing and dance... and dream!"

"You mean, you're going," said Jodie.

"Yes, I must. But I won't forget your gift, I promise. Wherever you are, I'll find you."

The Dream Snatcher tapped his feet *tappity tap* and suddenly he was gone.

Jodie ran and looked out over the ledge round the car park wall. She watched as the Dream Snatcher danced his way down the street, sometimes singing and sometimes playing a tune.

"Goodbye," she called after him. She could hear the people celebrating below.

"He's gone!" they cheered. "Our town is safe!"

Excitedly, Jodie raced down to tell what had happened.

"There you are, Miss!" said her uncle. "You saw sense at last. You sold him your dreams."

"And quite right too," chorused the people.

"He didn't need my dreams. He dreams his own now," said Jodie. She decided, after all, to leave it at that.

"You didn't get your cups of gold coins?" they quizzed her.

Jodie shook her head.

"You lost out there, Miss," the people tut-tutted. "You should have taken his offer when you had the chance."

"It's not just her that's lost out," said her uncle. "I'm stony broke. I'll have a night's kip, then it's back to work."

Everyone else was in the same position. All over the town it was work, work, work! No one had money to spare for extras. After a while, the shopping centre was boarded up. It fell into decay and they decided to bulldoze it to the ground.

Jodie looked on as the car park crashed down. She thought of the Dream Snatcher and wondered if he'd ever come back. Once she'd ventured to ask her uncle. He'd silenced her with a look and she didn't ask him again. But he never scolded her now. Her cousins didn't tease her and no one in the town made fun of her. Even so they kept her at a distance. She was glad when she was old enough to leave.

Jodie went abroad to study and travel and worked to pay her way. She went on to earn a good living and buy a house of her own. It was far from the town, a house with a stream nearby, and she loved it.

One morning there was a knock at the door. She ran to answer it. A man stood on the step. Before she could ask who he was or what he wanted, he handed her a small round box.

"It's for you," he said.

She saw the words *For Jodie* sparkle across the top. Quickly, she opened the box. Inside was a single pearl circled about with gold. The pearl shone with a soft white glow and specks of light of all different colours shimmered brightly through.

"It's wondrous, like the Dream Box," she murmured.

The Dream Snatcher had kept his promise. She'd never been sure if he would but if so, she'd always imagined he'd bring her the gift himself. Instead, he'd sent someone else.

"Well, that's that," thought Jodie. She turned to go indoors. But a question leapt into her mind. She must have an answer at once! She ran down the path and called the man back.

"Please, where is the Dream Snatcher? Can you tell me where I can find him?"

The man tapped his feet, *tappity tap*.

He took a silver flute from his pocket and played a few notes.

"Don't you know me, Jodie?"

Jodie stared, astonished. The Dream Snatcher was hugely tall as she remembered him, and fierce and wild-eyed. The man before her was certainly tall and as she looked again, she saw a look in his eye that though not exactly wild or fierce told her, yes, it was the Dream Snatcher!

"You once asked my name, Jodie. Remember?"

"Yes, I remember," said Jodie.

"My name is Kell," he said.

Jodie smiled. "I prefer Kell to the Dream Snatcher!"

"As the Dream Snatcher I was a monster. How I became one is a long story. One day I'll tell you," said Kell. "But now..." He gestured towards the gift he'd brought her.

"Do you like it, Jodie? Yes or no?"

He tried a smile but she saw he was anxious, and didn't pause for her answer.

"I like it very well," she said.

"Is that what your gran would have said!"

They laughed and Kell held out his hand and Jodie took it. They danced down the street, *tappity tap*. The

neighbours joined in too.

And in the town, the people suddenly found themselves

singing!

dancing!

making music!

Alf the Butcher banged a drum-saucepan and sang and danced all at once.

They puzzled about what had come over them. They'd never had such fun and things changed for the better - but they never rebuilt the shopping centre.

They filled in the site with flowers, trees, swings for the children, even a fountain.

Now it's a peaceful place in the heart of the town and they call it The Dream Snatcher's Garden.

Order Form

To order direct from the publishers, just make a list of the titles you want and fill in the form below:

Name ....

Address ....

....

....

Send to: Dept 6, HarperCollins Publishers Ltd, Westerhill Road, Bishopbriggs, Glasgow G64 2QT.

Please enclose a cheque or postal order to the value of the cover price, plus:

UK & BFPO: Add £1.00 for the first book, and 25p per copy for each additional book ordered.

Overseas and Eire: Add £2.95 service charge. Books will be sent by surface mail but quotes for airmail despatch will be given on request.

A 24-hour telephone ordering service is available to holders of Visa, MasterCard, Amex or Switch cards on 0141- 772 2281.

Collins
An *Imprint* of HarperCollins*Publishers*